Victoria's PANDEMONIUM

BY CRYSTAL LYN

ISBN: 978-1-4357-6285-5
ISBN (ebook): 9781458332622

Lulu Publishing 2022

DEDICATION

I would like to dedicate this book to the people of the world, to the ones we have lost, and to the ones who have a story to tell. The strong and the brave, the ones who speak up, and aren’t afraid to walk the path alone.

Love Coco

CHAPTER ONE

Turning Green

It was that time of year again when Miami turned into the South Pole...but with 80-degree weather, and your local Santa Claus wore red shorts and a tank top at the local mall. I just loved this time of year. Thanksgiving is fantastic - who doesn't enjoy an overwhelming amount of food, followed by a food coma that no one can get you out of? But, somehow, turkey day passed by so fast. And then began those four weeks of Christmas music on every station and debating if you're staying local or traveling. And, of course, the major flow of tourists that enter Miami can spice up the city.

I enjoyed everything about Christmas except for one thing, and that was Christmas shopping. Thankfully, I didn't have a major list, so I kept it simple online shopping and gift cards for my co-workers. Technically, it was just my Mom and Desi I shopped for and, well, there was no special man in my life. For the last few months, I had gone on some dates but nothing past that. Honestly, it was what I needed! I focused on myself, and my work/life balance was perfect. My best friend was still my best friend, but I was sharing with her now - my BFF had a boyfriend. Thankfully, I liked him. Josh was a good fit for Desi;

they have been dating for a few months now. What a shocker he is not a flight attendant. They met at the gym where he had been her trainer. I knew there was a reason she was working out so much!

I had spent two full weeks flying and staying in hotels and, now the weekend was coming up. It would be nice to have a few days off. I had plans to decorate the house, put up my tree, and enjoy some homemade coquito my Mom made. The delightful taste of cinnamon and coconut always hits the spot. It was Friday afternoon, and I was at home prepping my decorations with some jolly music playing lightly in the background, when my phone began to ring. It was Desi.

"Hey girl, what's up?"

"Hey Vic, nothing much - just waiting for Josh to stop by with some sushi! What are you up to?"

"Well, now I am untangling these Christmas lights on the couch."

"Vic... have you been watching the news at all?", Desi said.

"Um, Desi, you know I don't watch TV like that. It's always so depressing. Why? what's going on?"

Desi's tone had changed, "Well, there's, like, this virus in China that's doing major damage. The reports are scary."

"Oh, ok... wow. That does sound scary!" I exclaimed. "But, Desi, I'm sure we are ok. That is so far away! And you know the news is just to scare us, turn it off and wait for Josh on your porch. Get some fresh air...Desi do you hear me?"

"Yes, Victoria, I am currently nodding my head"

"Ok good! Give me a call later?"

I sat on my couch with tangled lights on my lap. Frustrated, I decided I would just go to the store and get a new set. I threw on my shoes, tied my hair up, and took a stroll to the store a few blocks away. It was so sunny today, with a slight breeze. I got to the store and went to the Christmas aisle. AH, there we go! Beautiful, untangled lights. I grabbed two packs and went to the cashier. I was fourth in line when I overheard the couple in front of me talking about the virus, and how there were reports of it in Italy. I felt my anxiety kicking in, and I just wanted to pay and get home. Fifteen minutes later, I was back home in the living room, putting up the lights, and slightly buzzed. I felt content and safe. My house was beginning to look festive!

Suddenly, there was a knock at my door, and I wasn't expecting anyone. As I walked to the door, I could see the reflection. It was my mother, what was she doing here?

"Hey mama, are you ok?"

"Yes, mija!" she said, "I was bored and decided to surprise you and cook dinner!" And she walked in with all her cooking utensils.

I could never say no to my mother's cooking, so off she went to the kitchen.

"Wow, Victoria, the place looks great! I'll help you put the tree up after dinner."

Mom was making baked chicken tonight with rice, beans, and avocado. I decided to take a break from decorating and chat with Mom while she made dinner. I always went over my plans with her: I knew she enjoyed talking about what I was up to, and it helped me to make sure I didn't miss anything. I had two work trips coming up and had to make sure I packaged my *stuff* right. Both strands were doing great, and all my dealers were doing their jobs brilliantly. It was smooth sailing. After dinner, I enjoyed a cup of coffee with Mom; but I was tired, so I decided to put the rest of my decorations up tomorrow. Off into my room, I went. Mom had decided to spend the night, so she made a bed on the couch, and put on her novela. I was lying in bed, listening to music, and scrolling on social media. Ugh, again I was seeing posts about this virus, so I gave in and googled what was going on around the world with this. Thankfully, there were no cases in the US yet, and there was a prediction that there would not be any cases. It was under control. That info made me feel a little better, but I was terrified of what was going on across the seas. *I think it's time for a nice bubble bath,* I thought; so, I filled the tub and dropped in my favorite CBD bath bomb. I added a second one for good measure - I needed extra relaxation. I followed this with some relaxing music, and a joint of my finest strand, *Calypso.* I slowly dipped my toes into the warm water that was infused with rose oil and lavender and, finally, I was fully consumed. Inhaling in and out, I hit my joint and rested my head on my bath pillow. I could feel the tension leaving my body. Just me, in my safe space, repeating affirmations of positivity. Putting me first. I soaked until my fingers and toes pruned, and I had my last hit. I massaged my skin with lotion, put on my PJs, and got into bed. I turned on my galaxy lights, spoke to my guardian angels, gave thanks to everything in my life, and off I went into dreamland.

I had awoken on Saturday morning to the smell of French toast, and my Mom listening to some salsa music in the kitchen. I rolled over, put on my cute unicorn slippers, went into the living room; and, to my surprise, my tree was up! I felt like a kid again.

"Hey, honey! I hope you don't mind, I put up the tree!" Mom said, "I couldn't sleep last night, so I went ahead and did it."

"I love it, Mom! Thank you! It looks so pretty!"

After breakfast, Mom had left, and Desi was stopping by. I didn't have much on my agenda for this Saturday. It was cloudy out today and, I guess, you could say it was a chilly day - mid-60s. Desi arrived with some empanadas and a bottle of wine.

"Hey, Vic! The place looks great! So festive!"

"Thanks, Des!" I said, "How was your night with Josh?"

"Nice! We had sushi, went to the mall, then just hung out at the house watching movies. I also was going over next week's trips. I have three coming up, how about you?"

"I've only got two coming up, luckily. One is to Atlanta, which is perfect so I can meet up with Neal and give him this month's product. The second trip is to Wyoming, and after that, I have two days off, so I have to fly over to California to do another drop. The airports have been crazy with everyone traveling for the holidays and, of course, you never know what to expect when planes are full."

As I took a big gulp of my wine, Desi giggled, "I hear ya, Vic!"

Saturday had come and gone, and now it was Sunday - laundry day and going over my final plans for this week. I was flying out to Atlanta tomorrow, so I had to get everything ready. I got a text from Neal confirming everything. Neal was a good person to have on my team. I was sitting on the floor of my closet in my room going through some stuff when my phone started to ring. It was an unknown number. Hesitant, I picked it up.

"...Hello?"

There was a woman on the phone with a Russian accent.

"Is this, Victoria?"

"Yes, it is. Who is this?"

"Hi, my name is Silvia. I am Henry's fiancé" "Oh! Hi!" I exclaimed.

I was a little confused. I hadn't heard from Henry in over a year. Furthermore, he had a fiancé? I heard a sniffle, and I became anxious.

"I was going through Henry's phone contacts and calling everyone on here. My Henry passed away two days ago."

I gasped. My heart was now pounding. With confusion, I stuttered, "...How?"

"He caught that awful virus. We had been vacationing in Italy for the last two months. He wanted a break from city life, so we found a cute cottage in a little village. It was beautiful. We even thought about moving there. Every night, we had this blissful routine of enjoying delicious food and wine and taking walks. We also were planning our wedding for the summer. About two weeks ago he started not feeling well; then, I became ill as well. We went to the doctors and were told it was just a virus and to get plenty of rest. The local people in the village had made this herbal tea, and within a few days, I started to feel better. But Henry did not. Eventually, he was taken to the hospital I cannot even talk about his last few days." Her voice became shaky, "He passed away with me holding his hand and me telling him I loved him. It was that virus that took the love of my life away. They ended up doing a few tests and he was positive for it."

With tears rolling down my face, I got up from the floor of my closet and went to the kitchen. I dropped some THC drops into my water and guzzled it.

"I am so sorry, Silvia. Henry was a good man. Is there a funeral I can help you with?"

"No, they are telling me I cannot even have a funeral for him, just cremation. I am flying back to the city with his ashes and having a memorial for him I would love for you to attend."

"Of course, Silvia. And if there's anything else I can do, please let me know. I look forward to meeting you."

I hung up the phone and burst into tears. I then called Desi to tell her the awful news. About a week later, I met Silvia in New York for Henry's memorial service. It was beautiful, and still so shocking.

I had done the same-day flight, so I was back in Miami that night. I just kept thinking about the last time I saw him as he smoked a cigar in my house when we ended our business together. I lit a white candle for him and knew I had an angel watching over me. I was all cried out, so I smoked a joint, and off to bed, I went. I could only have hope that there wouldn't be any more sadness. Who wants to be sad around the holidays?

CHAPTER TWO

Nochebuena

It was Christmas Eve. The night sky was clear, the air was crisp, and my house smelled delightful. My Mom had a roast in the oven and was making her delicious side dishes to go with it. I invited some of my co-workers over to play some games and have a few drinks. Desi would be stopping by with Josh as well. I hoped she'd like the gift Mom and I got her: a full day at the spa, with the best amenities you could imagine, at the best spa in the South Miami area. She was so excited to make an appointment.

As some of my friends started to show up, the Christmas spirit kicked in with music playing and drinks flowing, and I had my patio lit up for smoke breaks. The party was going well, and I felt the coquito kicking in, so I began dancing in the middle of my living room. Desi joined in, and we could not stop smiling and laughing. I must have danced for three songs in a row, and I was starting to sweat - I knew it was time for a break. I grabbed a joint and a drink and went to my patio.

My friend Lizzy was out there with her plus one and was just finishing her cigarette.

"Hey Victoria!" Lizzy called from across the patio, "Great party thank you for inviting me! This is my friend Tracy!"

"Hey, Tracy. Nice to meet you! Thanks for coming!"

We chatted for a few minutes, and they went back in. I was alone, sitting on my chair. It was so quiet outside, but the echo of laughter and music was gleaming from the windows of my house. I looked up into the sky. The moon was full, the sky was clear, and with holiday aroma, I took a deep breath in and let it out. How glorious was this? I was so thankful.

Snapping me back to reality, my phone started to ring. Hmmm, this was not a saved number. The area code was Virginia I picked it up.

"Hello?"

"Hey Victoria, it's Jacob. Merry Christmas"

I had looked at my phone it was midnight on the dot. Extremely shocked, and overcome with a sense of nausea, I opened the patio door to walk into my backyard - I couldn't stay still. It was literally a year since I'd heard from Jacob after he broke my heart. That was a really hard pill to swallow. I spent months binging on wine and ice cream, and there were so many nights I wanted to text him furious messages. Glad I didn't. I probably would have been texting some elderly woman insane things. I giggled out loud with that thought. Quickly I snapped back into the awkward moment I was in.

"Jacob…this is a surprise. Merry Christmas! Is this your new number?"

"Yes. Well, I've had it for about seven months."

Interesting, I thought to myself.

"…Oh, ok. Cool…It's a VA number, don't tell me you moved to Virginia." I nervously giggled thinking, he would say no.

"Ah…well, yes, I did. I decided to change it up! I like it out here. It's different from Colorado but in an effective way. Plus, the real estate business has been good to me."

"That's really good, Jacob," I sighed, "Well, I'm still out here in Miami doing what I do best. But I can't help but wonder, Jacob, why the call now?"

"Well, I guess you don't remember last Christmas? We spent it together and, well, I'm just sitting here in front of my fireplace having a drink and the liquor gave me the courage to call you."

Oh yes, I remembered that Christmas we spent together in his place making passionate love and eating take-out food. How could I forget?

"Well, I'm actually hosting a party right now. I should get back to my guests."

"Oh, yes, of course. Well…save my number and give me a call sometime when you can talk. Enjoy your night Victoria, it was nice to hear your voice."

"Same to you, Jacob."

He hung up and I stood there for a second, just listening to the hum of the dial tone, before going back into my house. Desi sauntered up to me.

"Hi!! Where have you been Vic?"

"I was out on the patio having a smoke and guess who called me?"

"…Who?" Desi whispered.

"Jacob!" I exclaimed.

“What in the world Vic? Why? It’s been at least a year since you’ve heard from him!”

“I know, I know. But he did give me some fascinating info like, he doesn’t live in Colorado anymore, among other things.”

“…Anyways!” exclaimed Desi, awkwardly, “Change of subject! Let us exchange gifts!”

We all gathered in the living room as we celebrated Noche Buena. The night was ending, my guests were leaving, and it was down to Mom, and Desi who was spending the night, along with my friend Patty who had a little too much to drink. I made her a bed on my couch, and Mom made a bed in my office, and Desi slept with me. We both lay there, engulfed by the noise of my ceiling fan, looking up at the galaxy stickers I had stuck to my ceiling.

“Good party tonight, Vic,” Desi whispered as I lay there and ran my fingers through my hair.

“I agree Desi, thank you. So, did Josh get you something good?”

“Oh my God, yes!” she shrieked as she shot up in my bed, “I didn’t want to wear it tonight but…here is a picture!”

The blinding light of her phone hit my tired eyes and revealed a stunning Tiffany tennis bracelet.

"Wow, Desi, that is so pretty!"

Shortly after, we both fell into a gorgeous slumber. I had one last thought before I went off into dreamland, and that was of Jacob.

The morning had arrived, and it was Christmas Day! Mom was already up making coffee and a light breakfast and had done some cleaning from the party. Patty was painfully hungover, but the coffee brought her back to life. The morning was accompanied by a nice breakfast joint that we passed back and forth. Shortly after, Patty left. It was already 1:30 PM when Desi awoke.

"Oh shit!" Desi yelped, "I have to get going! We're supposed to be heading to Josh's family's house in Fort Lauderdale! There's a guest room, so we're spending the night."

I gave Desi a tight hug, and off she went.

It was just me and Mom. I felt bad because there was no one at home waiting for her. My Mom has not dated anyone in ten years, the clock was ticking. I tried encouraging her to sign up to those dating sites; but she watched too many forensic files and, well, that was not an option. She had a few friends, but they were all married so they usually get together only once or twice a month. That was it for Mom. Oh, and I cannot forget her bingo nights at the YMCA - she had a surprisingly good winning streak! She always invites me to the games, but I usually end up making weird excuses. I am not at that level where bingo becomes entertaining yet. I was quietly on a mission to find her a partner this New Year. But today, Mom and I enjoyed the day at home, just watching TV and having the leftovers that she whipped up into a delicious soup. She had to leave early the next morning for her hair appointment nearby.

I had one more day off before I started work again and back to the business, I had a drop to do in LA. The last seven days of the year are so weird. You never know what to do with yourself. It's like a big pimple that, with every passing day, edges closer to popping. So, there I was, sitting alone in my closet and 1 AM, randomly trying things on (what else is there to do?), when I reached my hand to the very back and grabbed an old shoebox from my shelf. I opened it only to find all the sexy lingerie outfits I used to wear for Jacob. I totally forgot I even had this, let alone hid it here. Ugh.

Jacob loved when I dressed up. His favorite was this schoolgirl outfit that lay on the top of the box. I had gained a few pounds since we dated, but it was all in the right places. Two minutes later, there I was in full schoolgirl gear, standing in the mirror. Oh, the memories. And damn, I still looked good. I twirled and posed in the mirror admiring my new shape. I couldn't deny I wanted to send a picture to Jacob, and my heart started to race. My mind started to spiral.

What if he does not respond until tomorrow?

The whole point was to get a reaction now, not hours later!

What if I'm totally misreading and it's super awkward?

The more I thought about it, the less I wanted to do it. But… what if? Well, what the hell. I took a few pictures plopped on my stomach on my bed and examined each one. After a while, I found the perfect, added a cheeky winking emoji, pressed send, and hurtled my phone on the bed, and squealed.

Only minutes later, I heard my phone go off. I was afraid to look as if I was being watched. I grabbed my phone and went straight to the message. There were multiple emojis that could only translate that he liked the picture, followed by another message: *Oh, I remember that outfit* ;).

Why was I reading it in his voice? I squeaked again, this time with a cheesy grin. Oh wow, this has been the most excitement

I have had in months. I replied to him: *yea, I found our play outfits and I remembered this was your favorite one.* He replied immediately: *Well, you look great, as always.*

Mission accomplished! We began a small conversation and, yes, I was still in the outfit lying in bed. He said he wanted to call me tomorrow so we could talk!! *Oh boy, let me think about that...* I texted mischievously, before immediately following with: *Sure! Any time after 8 would be good for me :)*

He wished me good night, and we left it at that. I didn't want to give too much thought to what he wanted to talk about, so I distracted myself by slipping out of my seductive outfit, putting them all away back up in the corner of my closet, and getting into bed. I woke in the morning with about two hours until I had to report to the airport, cutting it close as usual! I made sure my package was nestled safely in my bag for my drop- in LA, started my getting ready playlist, and it was go time. I always get my bag and things together first and leave it at the door, with my purse and keys right there so I can grab them and go. I grabbed my lunch for the road: a delicious chicken salad, pita chips, and a bag of dark chocolate-covered blueberries.

Then it was time to put myself together. I always go for the clean and polished look when I'm working, so I slicked my hair back and twirled my long hair into a neat bun, leaving out one braided piece to wrap around it. Clean, fresh, natural makeup with a subtle mauve lip, and dewy cheeks. I slipped into my uniform, being careful not to destroy my pantyhose. I cannot *begin* to tell you how many pairs I have gone through. I usually bring at least three extra pairs with me whenever I fly just as a safety precaution for any wardrobe malfunctions. Final touches with light scented perfume and my red ruby studded earrings. In record time, I was ready to go and was just waiting for my driver to arrive.

Luckily, there wasn't too much traffic heading to the airport and, once I arrived, I just had to check through security and wait to board the aircraft. I always feel like the queen bee of security when I waltz in. They all knew me, so I never felt a sense of danger when I was carrying my packages. I stood in line and flashed an innocent smile as my turn came. I approached Lucas, head of security.

"Hey, Lucas!"

"Hey, Vic! Where are we going today?"

"I am heading to LA, actually." I chatted as my bag went through.

I stepped through the security machine, said hello to Cheryl as she did a light pat-down, and complimented my earrings. I grabbed my bag and told them all to have a lovely day and skipped on to my gate. I always made a stop into this one little pastry shop in the terminal that had the best pastries. My favorite was this vanilla bread, filled with this sweet pudding that was so soft and squishy, and paired perfectly with an iced coffee with oat milk, of course.

I sat down in my seat and started making my LA checklist when my phone vibrated. It was Jacob reminding me to call him tonight once I got settled into my hotel room. I replied simply with a *K* and smile emoji. What could be so important?

Okay, later I can play drug queen. Now, it's time to get into Victoria flight attendant mode. I welcomed the passengers with my bubbly smile and pointed them towards their seats. Luckily it wasn't a full flight, so it didn't take long before we were fully boarded. As passengers put their belongings away and buckled in, the captains were doing what they do best in the cockpit. Captain Liam was a veteran I'd had the pleasure of working with before. He was accompanied by a semi-new badass captain, Elizabeth. She was only twenty-eight and she'd been flying for about two years already, but had only been with our company for six months. It was refreshing to have a new face on board. She had spirals of brown curly hair she wore neatly in a bun. Her eyes were a piercing shade of hazel brown, and she was around the same height as me.

It was finally go time. I was sitting in my jumper seat making faces to my co-worker as we lined up with the runway. It doesn't matter how long you've been doing this job; adrenaline always kicks in when those engines kick in and you go rocketing down the runway and take flight.

Before I started the beverage and food services, I noticed Jacob had sent me a cute meme. I smirked and put my phone away.

The flight was going smoothly and, before I knew it, servicing and trash collection was over. Now we had about an hour to chill before landing. I was chatting with my colleague Amanda about all sorts of random things that made the hour go by because the next thing I knew, we were preparing for landing. Landing in LA always gave me mixed feelings because of the past drama.

After everyone was off the plane, the crew and I waited for our shuttle to the hotel. It was a breezy mid-70s tonight, and I took a big whiff of the sweet LA air. Once I checked into my hotel room, I made sure my package was good to go for when I needed to meet my dealer in thirty minutes. When the time came, I headed to the hotel lobby and spotted Elizabeth at the hotel restaurant enjoying a meal.

"All alone I see?"

"Yes. Just having a bite before bed." she said, with a flash of a smile, "And where are you heading to?"

"Oh, just to see some friends for a little!"

"Nice, have fun!"

I waved goodbye as I got into my taxi, and texted my dealer that I was on the way. We took a route through North Hollywood on the way there, and I couldn't stop thinking about all the crazy things I went through here, and how glad I was that it was over. The car pulled up to Milano's apartment. Although he was new to the crew, he had proven himself trustworthy, and responsible. Milano was super built: he was all about health and gave me a few good pointers on healthy eating. I'd recently become interested in making marijuana butter and oil for cooking. I tried it once at a pop-up restaurant and it was genuinely one of the best times I have ever had. There's nothing like leaving a meal high and stuffed. I was interested in learning more about this, and I had a feeling Milano might be a great fit for that business expansion. We had a small chat, I gave him the

Calypso, and collected this month's earnings. I wished Milano a happy early New Year and got a ride back to my hotel.

I was a little late on calling Jacob. I wasn't sure if he would still be awake, but I called anyway. Curled up, relaxed in bed, with a beautiful view of the sunset from my hotel window, I dialed.

"Well, hello!" he answered, surprised, "Didn't think you were going to call."

"Yeah, sorry I forgot the time difference. So, what up?"

"Well, I'm currently just working on some stuff. I know this is awkward, but do you want to FaceTime?"

I pondered for a second before deciding. Why not? I picked up the FaceTime and tried desperately to hide how nervous I was by slapping on a cheesy smile. Plus, my room was half dark by now. Jacob was looking good - there was no denying that. I felt my heart racing and my stomach bubbling.

"You look great, Vic"

"Thanks." I mumbled, "So, what did you want to talk about?"

He cleared his throat, "Well I know it's been a year since I've seen you, but I'm going to be in town for New Year to see my family, and I was wondering if you wanted to get together? Actually, I'm giving you an open invitation if you want to come by the party."

"Wow, thanks. I appreciate that. I don't have anything planned so that might be okay."

"Cool I was hoping you would say that!" he said, sounding relieved, "So how was your day?"

"It was decent! Worked, worked, and worked lol. I fly to New York tomorrow, then back home for a few days. I won't have my new fly schedule until after the first."

As we chatted more, it felt like old times. He had me giggling and feeling so free, just like he always did. We talked for nearly an hour before saying good night. As I lay in bed thought about how we ended things. How heartbroken I was. I didn't want to get ahead of myself again, so I turned off the overthinking that was going on in my head and went to bed. New Year was days away, and I was thankful to have had a pretty good year, and I had positive vibes that this year would be even better.

CHAPTER THREE

Pandemonium

It was two days away from New Year's Eve, and I was giving my house a deep clean. It was good luck to go into a new year with a totally spotless house. While I was at it, I started going through things I could donate to my local thrift shop. I wasn't having a party at my house this year since I had multiple invites to various very-important parties - the main one being Jacob's. Desi was having a party at her house so I figured Mom and I would do the count down there, and then I would head over to Jacobs. It was best to do it that way. How awkward would it be for the clock to strike twelve and kiss the person that broke my heart a year ago like nothing happened? Not to mention not seeing him for a full year. I'd also be a few drinks in, which would make things a lot smoother. I had the perfect outfit picked out. I decided to go all out and hire a makeup and hairstylist to make me extra glamorous. Obviously, I wouldn't be doing all of this if he wasn't around, but I had to look my best! I needed to show him exactly what he gave up.

I was in my kitchen listening to the radio when they started to talk about this virus again. I thought we were over this drama. Now there might be a confirmed case in the States - not exactly what I wanted to hear. Whelp! Off the radio went: I did not want that type of energy on my mind.

I wanted to go for a nice meal, but Mom was at bingo, and Desi was with Josh; so, solo I was! Oh well, out to dinner alone. The place I decided on was near the beach, so the view was breathtaking as I arrived at the restaurant. I asked for outdoor dining, and the server gave me this cute little nook next to a palm tree where I could watch the sunset on the water, and she lit a candle on the table. How cute was this setup? I was already hungry, so I ordered an appetizer and a mojito to start. As it drifted into the dark, I enjoyed the view and the candlelight alongside my mojito; but naturally, I had no choice but to start couple watching. It was fun to watch couples and I love to make up stories about them; but, before I could get too invested, my main course arrived. Crab cakes, with a spring salad drizzled in balsamic vinegar – delicious. I grabbed dessert to go, a nice slice of strawberry cheesecake, which would be a perfect nighttime snack.

When I arrived home, there was a package waiting by the front door. I hadn't ordered anything, so this was a surprise. It was a medium brown box which I plopped the package on my table the moment I got inside. No name. This was suspicious. I opened it up and peered inside. Wow. I pulled out the most beautiful, sparkling dress with matching heels, and a card that read:

from, Jacob x

I was completely speechless, and the dress was *gorgeous*. I immediately FaceTimed Desi to show her the outfit, and we both freaked out with excitement at what this could mean. I didn't know whether to text or call Jacob, but I plucked up the courage and called him. The phone rang for a moment, and he picked up.

"Hello, Victoria. How are you?"

"Hello, Jacob!" I giggled anxiously, "That was extremely sweet of you and totally off guard."

"You are more than welcome. Do you really like it though?"

"I literally love it!" I exclaimed.

"Perfect! I can't wait to see you in it on New Year's Eve!"

My whole body was flustered, and I was tingling all over.

"I'm coming over around twelve-thirty if that's cool. I'll be at Desis for the ball drop with my Mom, then I'll head over to your cousin's house."

"Sounds good, Vic. I cannot wait to see you."

We hung up, and I was smitten. I went to bed that night, filled with enthusiasm and blissful thoughts.

I woke in the morning to the Florida sun beaming in through my window. What a beautiful day it was! I planned to spend the day getting pampered and ready. I had a manicure and pedicure appointment, and I stopped at my local coffee shop on the way for my classic ice coffee, extra sweet, with almond milk. The nail salon was busy, but my nail tech, Rose, was all set up waiting for me. Rose had been my nail tech for about two years, and I really enjoyed our sessions. She always did a fantastic job, and it was like a free therapy session with all the topics we'd cover! After pampering the day away, and feeling wonderfully refreshed, I picked up some delicious chicken soup from a restaurant close to my house. When I got home, I put my food on the table, kicked off my sandals, and tossed my hair out of the way into a bun.

One thing I can say I sure miss coming home to is Lucy. I lost her a few months ago because of an ongoing kidney condition she had. She was suffering, so I had no choice but to put her to rest. Her paw print and ashes were in pride of place on a stand in my room. I wasn't ready to get a new cat, but I just felt guilty every time I thought about it.

I slumped onto the couch turned on my favorite show about four brilliant older women. It's crazy how much I loved the show considering I was so young at the time it was out. There was something about those four women that gave me comfort. The fact that they lived in Miami made it even better, and I always joked around saying that if I never got married, or my husband passed away, this is how I'd want to live out the remaining years of my life. One of them was in her late nineties and still kicking. That was so inspiring to me. I devoured my soup with a hunk of bread and was stuck on the couch. Luckily, I had a joint on the table. I lit it up and felt my body melt.

Tomorrow was the big day! I had a hair appointment, and my makeup artist was coming to my house in the afternoon. I was going to call it a night as tomorrow I was sure I wouldn't get any sleep! I dimmed my pink Himalayan salt lamp, grabbed my cozy blanket that was draped over my couch, and fell into a deep sleep.

I awoke in the morning with a big yawn and a stretch. Today was New Year's Eve! I had butterflies fluttering in my stomach. I made some home fries with peppers and onions and iced coffee, before heading off to my hair appointment. I was re-touching my color, getting a deep hair mask, a trim, and a blowout with some curls. My hair had grown so much in the last few months, so I knew the style would be perfect for me. As usual, I chatted it up with my hairstylist. He had plans tonight to celebrate on a boat. I thought that was neat. I bet the fireworks would be beautiful from the water. A couple of hours later, I was done, and, wow. I looked good! One last spray and I was on my way home.

My makeup artist was coming over in a while to slay this face of mine, and I needed this face to look good all night. I hopped in the shower with my head completely wrapped, made sure to get all the right parts clean. Refreshed, I massaged my favorite cream butter moisturizer into my skin until I smelled like a tropical paradise kissed with sunlight. I threw on my robe, rolled up a joint, and smoked about half until I heard the doorbell.

Eliza arrived with a shit load of makeup. After setting everything up and fixing the lighting, she began her magic. Eliza was referred to me by a co-worker who used her for her wedding, so I trusted her with my look. She got straight to work. We were going for a sultry look, with a winged liner so sharp it could cut just looking at it. It was fun to talk to her and, of course, we talked about men. She told me something similar happened to her, like what happened to me. How many more of us were out there with broken hearts, going along with everyday life because we had to be resilient? After about an hour, my face was slain. I loved the look. She had done an excellent job; I would definitely hire her again. She had taken some pictures for her Instagram and portfolio and off, she went.

I blinked and it was 8 PM. Mom had just arrived at the house, and she looked so pretty in her long, golden dress. Her hair was curled, and her makeup was natural and glowy. We decided to have a drink together and reflect on the year before heading to Desi's party. We sat on my patio admiring the night sky as we sipped on our wine, and made New Year's resolutions for each other. Mine for her was to find a boyfriend. I just didn't want her to be lonely. And, well, for me, she wanted me to start making my own sofrito. It was a joke between us. We sipped the last drop of wine a little after 9 PM when the taxi had just pulled up to the house. Excitedly, we hopped into the taxi and headed to Desi's house. On the way there I received a text from Jacob. It was a picture of him in his suit, and a message that read: *can't wait to see you...* Wow did he look good. I felt butterflies in my stomach, and even though I was sitting, my knees felt weak.

Mom caught me smirking and asked: “Who is texting you?”

“Jacob” I replied.

“Oh, Victoria! The way you guys ended things last year!”

“I know, Mom! But he’s in town so I’m going to his party after the ball drops. You can stay at Desis, or I can make sure you get home safe.”

She gave me a look as any mother would do.

We finally got to Desis, and she had decorated her backyard beautifully. There were sparkling soft lights in between the palm trees, and she had ivy-colored table covers with a hint of golden glitter, and white roses at every table. I spotted Desi in her kitchen from the backyard. She even had a greeter to escort us, and he also served us some Champagne. Wow, my best friend looked so-- of course, she was matching with Josh-- but they looked cute!

“Everything looks beautiful bestie”

“Thanks, Vic!”

The night was turning out lovely. There was music, delicious food, and drinks, and everyone was having a wonderful time. I had to make sure I didn't get *too* drunk; but, regardless, I sure was going to use Desis room to clean myself up a little before I left her party. There were forty-five minutes left until the ball dropped, I felt nervous but excited.

Mom was having an exciting time! It was weird…I did not know if wishes were coming true for her. She had been introduced to Desi's uncle who lived in Palm Beach. He was a retired police officer, and he made beautiful outdoor furniture as a hobby now. They were having so much fun together dancing - I didn't even know my mom could move like that!

Ah! ten minutes left! Everyone, about forty guests (mostly couples), started to fill their Champagne glasses. We had all gathered in Desis's living room and turned on the TV, and there was New York Times Square. It was packed and full of life, and the famous ball was displayed on the screen. The last few minutes of the year were filled will small talk, but I kept my eyes on the TV.

Only four minutes left now. My heart was racing, partially because I knew that I would be seeing Jacob shortly. Mom stood next to me and introduced me to her new friend Ricardo.

He had pepper gray hair and bright blue eyes. I could tell Mom liked him. She was smitten!

One minute left. We started the countdown and with ten seconds to go, we started to yell

"TEN…NINE…EIGHT…SEVEN…SIX…FIVE… FOUR…THR EE…TWO…ONE… HAPPY NEW YEAR!"

Mom wrapped her arms around me we hugged and kissed. Then, she did the unthinkable. She kissed Ricardo on the lips! My eyes opened wide.

"Mother!!"

As he pulled her away, she giggled joyfully.

Well, it was go time! I headed to Desis's room to freshen up. I reapplied some deodorant, followed by her best perfume. Then, I rifled through her makeup bag to freshen up my face. Thankfully, she had extra toothbrushes, so I wouldn't have tequila breath…even though I had planned to take one more shot before I left. Jacob was already texting me asking me if I was on the way, and my heart was pounding. *Yes*, I replied, even though I was still grooming myself. Josh was going to drop me off; it was about a twenty-minute drive. I took one last look in the mirror, hugged Desi, and told her to look out for my Mom.

She would just spend the night there of course, and I knew Ricardo would be sleeping there too. I surely would be asking her tomorrow how the rest of her night went!

As we drove to Jacob's cousin's house, I couldn't help but think about the last time we were face to face. I was in tears, and his eyes darted with confusion. I was tipsy but still could feel all those emotions. I didn't want to drink to feel numb. I small talked with Josh from the passenger seat and, before I knew it, we were a couple of minutes away. Jacob said he would be waiting outside for me. I pulled out my phone to check myself. Josh kept telling me to stop fidgeting. Yeah okay, what did he know? As we pulled up to the side of the house, I could see him standing there in the driveway. Man did he look good - ugh! I got out of the car, and Josh pulled away. I couldn't look him in the face at first, so I kind of just giggled and looked down and the heels he'd given me. He hugged me tight and lifted me off the ground.

"Well, look who made it!" He said, with a smirk. "Come in!"

As I stepped inside the house, I was surprised to see only a few people; but, simultaneously, relieved. I guess most people had left to other parties or had gone home.

"Hey Vic, drink?" He murmured, with a hand on my waist.

"Sure! Shot of tequila if you have it."

His eyes opened wide: he remembered our wild tequila nights, and we toasted to health and joy for the coming year. I couldn't believe that I was with him.

Jacob introduced me to the people who were still at the party, and then we went out back. I had brought a joint with me, so I lit it up, and we had our first session of the year. Side by side, while we shared a joint, I still couldn't look into his eyes.

"I am so happy you decided to come," Jacob smiled. "You look so beautiful."

His eyes flitted from mine to the floor. He was nervous too.

"I know there must be so much you want to say to me; so, I'm ready."

"Ah…"

I was taken off guard. At this point, I really didn't think it was the right time to talk about our breakup. Not right now.

"You know what, Jacob. We always have tomorrow." I sighed, exhaling happy smoke. Surprised, he just nodded his head and flashed his killer smile.

Now what? I thought to myself. I assume he thought we were going to have some painful, gut-wrenching talk; but, with the alcohol and weed rushing through my system, I was not going to set myself up for failure and sadness. Instead, I let him do the talking. He told me what he'd been up to in the last year, and how much he liked living in Virginia now.

Two hours had passed it was 3:30 AM. Everyone was gone, and it was just me and him. Part of me wanted to just throw myself on him, but I didn't even know if he wanted me like that anymore. I didn't want to humiliate myself less than four hours into the new year! He offered me the guest room: obviously, I wasn't going to get a taxi at this time, so I said okay. He walked me to the guest room and gave me a hug at the door. How awkward was this? He also had given me a t-shirt of his to wear to sleep. It smelt like him. Not fair. I got into bed with the familiar noise of the ceiling fan. I lay there, staring up at the ceiling, way too wired to sleep. As if I willed it to happen, my phone had vibrated. *So, are you cozy?* Jacob said. Sweet! *Yes, but it could be better…* I replied, baiting. He replied with a seemingly oblivious question mark. A question mark? Really? I didn't even know how to respond, so I rolled over with frustration.

Moments later, the bedroom door had swung open. There he was. Nothing was said, and he got into bed. He began to kiss me and gripped my face, passionately. I ran my fingers through his thick hair: my biggest turn-on. We kissed slowly, gently. Every breath I took was consumed with him. I rolled on top of him and took off the shirt he'd given me. In just my thong, I leaned over and kissed his neck and his chest as he gripped my ass. Warmth was overflowing inside me, and I slipped my panties off. He put me on my back and softly kissed my bare breasts. I was floating. We began to move as one. With every pulsating thrust, I moaned. We fit together like a puzzle, and all I could think about was how I didn't want this to end. The sheets were coming off the bed from all the movement. Before we knew it, the birds were chirping and the first sign of the sun breaking through the moonlight appeared. Exhausted, but relaxed, I felt like I was laying on clouds. He held me in his arms as we fell asleep.

We awoke to a knock at the bedroom door: his cousin letting us know there was breakfast. What time was it, and where the heck was my phone? I rolled off the bed and onto the floor to excavate my phone from under the bed. I took a deep breath in and rubbed my tired, eyeliner- smeared eyes, not to mention one of my false eyelashes that was just chilling there on the floor. It was 9:45 AM. Ugh, only three hours of sleep and I felt like I was still drunk. As I pulled on my dress from last night, I wished I had some sweatpants and a t-shirt of my own to throw on. Jacob sat up and rubbed his stubbled face.

"Well, I have a splitting headache." He said, quietly. "I need some water."

We headed to the living room, where his cousin and his wife had prepared quite a spread; but my appetite was shot, so I just had some water, and these cut up strawberries and blueberries. After breakfast, I told Jacob I had to leave. I had to keep him wanting more!

"So, do you think I can come by your place tonight? If you don't mind, of course," he said, with a coy smile.

"Sure!" I yelped, in a poor effort to stay composed. "I'll be home around nine."

He walked me to my taxi, and kissed me on the lip, before giving me a cheeky smack on the butt. I couldn't wait to get home and shower, and call Desi, and check on my mother! I wonder how her night ended! I cringed to think it was the same way mine did.

When I arrived home, I peeled off my dress and jumped immediately into the shower. The warm water felt insanely good on my tired body. I got into some comfy clothes and checked in on Mom. Let's just say…she had a new friend. I called Desi, no answer. I ordered a huge sandwich and an iced tea from this amazing little sandwich place not too far from the house. As soon as it arrived, I devoured it and promptly passed out for 3 hours. I woke up to find multiple missed calls, and a text, from Jacob, making sure tonight was still on. I replied, *Yes!* with a wink emoji. I tried Desi again and she picked up. Thank God. I needed to talk to *someone* about last night! I gave her all the details, and she was shocked. Duh. But what shocked her the most was that he was coming over tonight.

I eventually got myself up from my bed and got myself together. I lightly curled my hair and did some chill makeup. I decided on a one-piece romper and sprayed my favorite perfume on my wrists and neck. I lit some candles and put on my twinkle lights to set the vibes.

As I relaxed on my couch, scrolling through my phone, there was a knock at my door. 8:30 PM on the dot, and he was here already. I opened the door, and there he was with flowers in his hand - they were beautiful. Flattered, I took them and folded him into a hug.

"You smell so good; I could just eat you!" he said and nibbled at my neck.

"Come in!" I giggled. "Have a seat! Drink?"

I wasn't nervous at all. Obviously.

"Sure, why not," he replied.

I poured us both a glass of red, turned on some music, and sauntered over to sit beside him.

"So…last night was fun." I said with a shy smile.

"Yes, it was." he said softly, as the smile dropped from his face. "But I came here to talk to you..."

My heart dropped into my stomach.

"Okay then. Talk. I'm listening."

"I know the way we left things off was horrible and then we went a full year without talking. But there were so many times I thought about you and wanted to reach out, but I could never follow through. I regret not trying with you."

I couldn't believe what I was hearing. It was like…I always envisioned this but never thought it would actually happen. A perfect, genuine apology. I also said to myself that, if this ever happened, I would be a bitch to him; but here I was, quiet as a mouse scurrying in the night. I took a deep breath in.

"What are you trying to say, Jacob?"

"I want to get back together. I know it would be long-distance, but I'm a lot closer now than I was before. I'm committed to making you mine again and forever this time."

"…I don't know, Jacob." I stuttered, "Last time, my heart was broken. You don't know how angry and hurt I was. Too many nights I lay awake replaying that day you told me that you didn't love me."

Wounded, he took a sip of his drink. "You don't have to give me an answer tonight, but I really want you to think about it things. It would be different this time."

We talked for about an hour about anything else I could think of to change the topic, before he told me he had to leave he had a 4 AM flight back to Virginia. I walked him to my door and he scooped me up. We blissfully kissed for a few minutes.

Snuggling his face into my neck, "Ah, I just want to smell you and have your scent on me before I leave!"

"Do you want me to spray you with my perfume?" I laughed as we kissed one last time. We said a meaningful goodbye, and I closed the door. I had a lot to think about indeed. There was no way in Hell he was going to break me again, in any way, shape, or form; but my heart desired him. To think this was just the first day of the year. What a way to begin it.

CHAPTER FOUR

Valentina

It had been a few weeks since my rekindling with Jacob, and we were talking on the phone and FaceTiming daily. Jacob wanted me to come out to see him and I figured why not? It might be nice to get away for a few days, and I definitely wanted to see his neck of the woods (AKA be nosey). So, we made plans for me to fly out for Valentine's Day weekend! How funny: last year, I was alone, bitter, and angry at Jacob, hoping that if he did have a Valentine, he got massive diarrhea at their romantic dinner and had to cut it short. Now, look at me going to see him! It really is funny how life works sometimes. Regardless, he would never know those miserable thoughts I had! I was going to remain optimistic that things would blossom between us.

I was making baked ziti for dinner, and Desi was coming over with some wine. Baked ziti was my specialty. Anyone I've ever made it for just loved it. I think it was my…special ingredient. Desi had arrived just as it was coming out of the oven, piping hot.

"Vic, it smells divine in here." Desi said with a huge inhale. "I also brought us some garlic bread from the bakery!"

We opened up the wine and sat at the table. I took a few sips as I waited for the food to cool off.

"So, Vic…what's new?"

"Well, you'll never believe it. I'm heading out to Virginia for Valentine's Day weekend to see Jacob!"

Desis widened, "Excuse me missy? You're really going out there?"

"Yes! I am! I want to see him, and his lifestyle, and I haven't been to Virginia in years. A lot of great reasons!

Stunned into silence, Desi gulped the rest of her wine. I'll be the one laughing when this trip just proves he's my man!

Dinner was amazing, and we were both stuffed and tipsy. The TV was playing, but we hardly paid any attention to it and carried on talking about my upcoming trip. I could sense Desi was getting bored of my gloating when she turned the channel to the news. She knew damn well I didn't want to watch that depressing stuff but, whatever. I was two glasses in.

More talk of the virus. It had reached the States. Although cases were minor, it was here. I wasn't sure how I felt about it, and I wondered, *would it get to Miami?* Desi and I went through two bottles of wine before blissfully passing out in my bed.

I was startled awake the next morning by a call from Jacob. "Hello, beautiful!"

"Hi, babe!" I sighed, scratching the crust off my lips. "I passed out last night with Desi. We totally stuffed ourselves with pasta, and then had a fair share of wine."

"Sounds like you had an exciting night!" he said, with a laugh.

As Desi started to wake up, she was moaning and groaning.

"Ugh, what a headache," she whined as she rolled back into burrito form.

Jacob and I chatted for a few golden minutes. He told me how happy he was that I was coming next weekend, and how lovely it was that Valentine's Day was on a Saturday.

After we hung up, I rolled out of bed to hop in the shower: I had some errands to do. I had the whole week off, so this week I was focusing on my garden and my trip to see Jacob. I was nervous, but excited. We hadn't slept in a bed together in such a long time. I remember when we first started that part in our relationship before. It was awkward. It's like, you can't *fully* be yourself in bed. Sometimes, our bodies do things when we are sleeping. Like, the first time I ever heard Jacob fart was in his sleep. I remember acting like I didn't hear anything, even though he literally farted himself awake. I tried desperately to act like I was still asleep, but I could not contain myself. He farted himself AWAKE!

After our first weekend sleepover, we became way more comfortable. It was funny because we didn't share the same blanket, he had his own and I had my own, and that was perfectly fine with me. We both liked our space when we were sleeping. We weren't that type of couple that smothered each other, but we *were* the type of couple to have sex multiple times a day. Not to brag. But, just like most couples, we had our pet peeves. I remember I could not stand when we would eat dinner and he would scarf his food down within minutes and leave me to eat the rest of dinner alone. At least he would still sit there and talk to me. I can tell you one of his peeves. Every night before going to sleep, I would rub peppermint oil all over me, which would leave a lingering aroma of menthol for at least an hour and made me untouchable. I usually applied my oil when I knew it was really *bed*time: it just made me feel so relaxed and soothed my muscles, even though it made his eyes burn, or whatever.

Thursday had finally arrived, and I was flying out at 6 AM on Friday morning. I spent the day packing and doing last-minute things I could think of. My mom was going to spend the weekend at my house, and her new friend Ricardo would be coming by. My Mom knew where I was going and just told me to be safe and have fun, which is funny because I told her the same thing. I went to bed early: I had to be up extra early since I was going in full glam. I had to look my very best, even if it meant getting up at 3 AM. Beauty is pain, after all! Before I knew it, my alarm was going off. I rolled over to text Jacob that I was awake and couldn't wait to see him. The butterflies in my stomach were getting the best of me, so I took a ginger pill to calm my nausea. An hour later, I was glammed up: a fresh blowout, and a perfectly polished face. I decided to wear this cute pink sweatsuit that said *barbie*. I said goodbye to my Mom, and off I went.

This was really happening! The airport was empty, but I still used my badge to get through TSA so, before I knew it, I was waiting to board my flight. The night sky was beginning to show signs of sunrise. I checked the weather in Virginia and, boy, was it cold. *Mid-40s partly cloudy,* but that was okay: I had sweaters packed and pants with these black cute boots. It was going to be fun to dress it winter clothes for a few days!

Once I boarded my plane, I texted Jacob one more time to let him know I would see him soon and my flight would be landing around 8:30 AM. He replied with a heart emoji, and my butterflies were back. Once we were in the air and stable, I asked for some hot tea which came with these half- dipped, almond topped biscotti. After that, I managed to doze off into a half-awake half-asleep nap. That made the time go by because, the next thing I knew, we had about fifteen minutes before landing. That was my time to refresh my face, use the bathroom, and get my thoughts together. Just like that, I was stepping off the plane. I could feel the cold already. I walked down to baggage claim and my eyes widened. There he was, standing there with flowers. I was in total shock: I figured he would just pull up outside when I was ready! He hugged me so tightly, and he smelled amazing.

"You look beautiful, Vic."

When my bag came out, he grabbed it for me and walked me to his car. The moment he grabbed my hand, my whole body was buzzing. I could only imagine what would happen once we got to his house. We talked non-stop the whole ride to his house, and I could barely stop smiling.

His house was really nice. Three bedrooms, one that he used as an office; two bathrooms; and a garage. His backyard practically spilled into the woods if you ignored the fence. That was my least favorite thing about the place – I thought it was just creepy, but he didn't mind it. After showing me to his room, I kicked off my shoes and lay on his bed. It was still so early! A few minutes later, Jacob came back in his PJs.

"Can I join?"

"Of course! I mean it's your bed after all!" I laughed. He put on some TV, closed the blinds, and snuggled into me.

"Are you cold, baby?"

"No, I'm good! It's toasty in here."

I fell into his eyes, and we began kissing. His lips were the same. Soft and breathtaking he then stopped for a moment and looked into my eyes.

"I missed you, mi amor."

I caressed his soft black hair and pulled him closer to me. I felt so content being back in his arms again; but at the same time, scared to trust him with my heart again. He had broken it once already, and badly. At the same time, none of that mattered. We were both naked, under the covers, consumed in scents of love and passion. We finished our lovemaking and I drifted into a nap. What a way to start our romantic weekend!

I woke up to Jacob on his phone, so I grabbed mine. It was 2:45 PM, I had slept for almost two hours. I was starving!

“Hey, you,” he said from the edge of the bed. “Welcome back! Are you hungry?”

“Yes! I was just thinking! I’m starving!” I replied.

“Okay, well let’s go get something to eat! I know some great places near here.”

I got up, changed my outfit, and texted my Mom and Desi: I hadn’t replied to their messages. But I did have my location shared with Desi, per her request. Now *that* was a good friend. Jacob took me to this cute restaurant, with a really great menu of appetizers. Naturally, we ordered a few different ones, a coconut mojito for me, and whisky on the rocks for him. The food was amazing, and his company – and that mojito - had me feeling fuzzy and warm. Jacob had a few drinks too, so he was just as happy. When we left the restaurant, we strolled around a little. He wanted to show me the area, and it was gorgeous! A ton of different restaurants and stores, including a few of my chain favorites. We made our way back to his place, where I changed right into some warm PJs. Of course, they were appealing; but also, very warm. I was not used to this weather. Jacob switched on his electric fireplace which set such a comfy vibe. We talked for hours about random stuff, simply enjoying each other. We laughed, and kissed, and eventually drifted off to sleep.

I awoke the next morning to sweet kisses on the back of my neck, and his warm body against mine. I could see where this was going, and I wanted him too. I told him to give me a second, and I ran to the bathroom. I hastily brushed my teeth, rinsed my face, and applied some scented lavender lotion to my body. I crawled back into bed, on top of him. I returned the kisses he gifted me, as he held me softly. This Valentine's Day was starting off nice. I ran my hand through his hair and grabbed his face, telling him who was in control. I slunk down towards him and knew how much he wanted me.

After our passionate wake-up call, we went to the kitchen and had bagels, with coffee for him, and tea for me. He revealed that he had a special day planned for us, complete with a romantic dinner. I was really excited about today. We got dressed and headed out to his first surprise.

We arrived at this polished-looking building and when we walked in, I realized we were at a spa. I love spas! He had booked us a couple's spa, then a mud bath, with Champagne, and chocolate strawberries! The spa was beautiful, and the amenities were amazing. There was a Himalayan salt room, steam sauna, and three different temperature tubs, not to mention - my personal favorite - the jade room. We ended up spending three glorious hours at the spa, and I left feeling so refreshed. Who could ask for anything more?

"So, Vic," Jacob said, with his signature smirk. "I have one more surprise just a few minutes away."

We pulled up to a jewelry store, and for a split second, I thought *is he going to propose?* What a silly brain I had. We went inside and were greeted by the owner.

"Hey, Jacob! Nice to see you, I've been waiting for you!"

"Victoria, this is my friend Allen! This is his jewelry store."

"Lovely to meet you!"

"Lovely to meet *you*!" he said, kissing my hand.

As I looked around, I fell in love with so many of the pieces. I particularly loved these delicate gem rings that he had on display. Allen went to the back of the store and returned a few minutes later with a box. He handed it to Jacob and winked. Phew, it wasn't a ring. It was in a long velvet box.

"Happy Valentine's Day, Victoria," Jacob said, softly. "I hope you like this."

He took the top off the box and unveiled a beautiful, rose gold necklace, with a crescent moon. He knew how much I loved the moon and stars. My face flushed as he put it around my neck.

"Oh, Jacob," I exclaimed. "This is really so beautiful and so thoughtful. Thank you!"

I folded him into a kiss.

On the way back to his house, he told me he had dinner reservations for us at one of his favorite restaurants.

"You know what? Cancel it," I said, going out on a limb. "lets just order something, grab a bottle of tequila, and stay home. I'm sure the restaurants are so packed. Plus, we can have fun at the house. Just you and me."

"You know what, that sounds really nice. Let's do it!"

We stopped at a convenience store and got the tequila, plus ginger ale, pineapple juice, and his classic small premium whisky. Once we got home, we lit some candles, and put the fireplace on, and looked online to see which restaurants were delivering. He pointed out this Italian restaurant he liked, so I decided on chicken and broccoli alfredo with garlic bread, and he got mussels in red sauce with pasta. I went ahead and rolled up a joint, and we smoked it in his living room. The vibe was so perfect right now. Jacob's house was cozy, and so was his company. I was bummed to leave tomorrow, but we had tonight and some of tomorrow to enjoy.

The food arrived and it was delicious. He had finished before me, and I didn't want to get too stuffed before I could give him a big thank you! After dinner, we relaxed a little and chatted, before deciding to play a little drinking game. Drink or strip. Whoever's turn it was had to either take a shot or take something off. This was going to get interesting, and fast. Jacob put on some sultry music and the game began. It didn't take long before we were drunk, half-naked, and dancing and all over each other. I was in the middle of his living room with a beer in my hand, singing and prancing around in my sexy lingerie. Jacob admired me from the couch. He had this smug smirk upon his face, and he couldn't keep his eyes off me - they followed me everywhere, and I loved it. Then, like fate, our song came on. I grabbed his hand and pulled him up to dance with me. I couldn't help but kiss him all over his face. Then he lifted me against the wall and slowly caressed my body, before pulling my hair. I was hot all over. We took one more shot, and he carried me to his bed.

We couldn't keep our hands off each other as we rolled around in his satin sheets.

"How about a shower?" he asked

"Ooh sure, why not!"

Jacob had a pristine, stone-tiled shower, with a really big shower head, and eucalyptus leaves hanging over the showerhead giving off its cool aroma with the steam of the shower. We got in and things began to steam up. Jacob tentatively, gently lathered up my wet skin, before he couldn't resist anymore. He pushed me up against the glass door of the shower and pulled me into his kiss. The water was hitting us, and the moment felt like heaven. We must have been in there for something like forty-five minutes, the water was beginning to get cold. We were squeaky clean and glowing. He gave me one of his plush robes and I flopped onto his bed with wet hair, and he handed me some water. I was so relaxed and refreshed, and I couldn't stop smiling, and neither could Jacob. We had the cheesecake that we ordered with our dinner, which really hit the spot, and then we both crawled into bed. I snuggled into the crook of his arm, and we both drifted off to sleep. *What a magical day,* I thought as I drifted off to sleep.

It was so nice to sleep in next to Jacob, but I was painfully sad that I had to leave tonight. My flight was at 6 PM, so at least we had the day together. The rain outside dampened our plans because Jacob wanted to show me around some more. I told him not to worry, I'd be back. We hung out at the house instead. You'd think we were sexed out, but we went for two more rounds before I really needed to start gathering my stuff. Before we knew it, it was time to leave. I turned around and waved goodbye to his adorable house.

Jacob laughed and said, "You'll be back, silly!"

He put my suitcase in the trunk and off we went. I felt myself becoming more and more anxious the closer we got to the airport. It had been such a great weekend, and it was as if we never separated in the first place. It was so beautiful, but also so scary, to have all these feelings back again. As we pulled up to the airport, my hands got sweaty. I told myself I wouldn't cry, there really was no reason to. I was just really going to miss him. No one was dying. I stretched my arms out for a hug, and he gripped me up off the ground spun me around.

"Te quiero mi Princesa," he said as he kissed my forehead. I leaned in and kissed his soft, luscious lips. I grabbed my suitcase and started to walk away. I couldn't help but look back, and he waved. My heart ached, but now I was on a mission to get home as fast as possible. I sure did miss the Miami weather.

CHAPTER FIVE

Pandemonium

A week had passed since I returned from Virginia. My weekend with Jacob was better than I could have ever imagined. Since I got back to Miami, we talked on the phone every day, and he already had plans to come out and see me towards the end of March. For the first time in so long, I was really, truly happy. Everything was going so well in my life. There was really nothing I could complain about. Well, I did have a busy week of work coming up. I was traveling to three different cities, and one of them I would be doing a drop of some Calypso. Desi was booked for one of the trips with me, to San Diego. I used to go there on some of my first work trips when I first became a flight attendant. I said I'd take the trip to help a fellow coworker who was sick. I figured, why not fly with my best friend, *and* spend a day in San Diego? I'm sure we could find something to do with our spare time!

It was a Thursday night, and I was currently comatose on my couch after some delicious tacos I picked up from this local stand. I was laying there, scrolling on my phone, when there it was again. That infamous virus, insulting my notifications with another headline. I held my breath and looked it up online.

I was shocked. It was showing up in more and more states… including Miami. I couldn't believe that this still was going on; or, maybe I just didn't want to pay attention. I read the article and, with every word, my distress grew. I threw my phone down and closed my eyes. I just lay there for a few minutes, desperately trying to silence the fear in my head. I decided to FaceTime Jacob – that would get my mind off it.

"Hey, Princesa!" he said with a smile that immediately brought me back to Earth, "How are you tonight?"

"I'm good, babe! Just had some great tacos and I was just relaxing on the couch until I read about this virus thing that's going on. I guess I've been so busy I thought it was under control, but now I'm reading that there are cases popping up all over."

"Yeah, Vic. People at the agency are talking about it every day now. I put a large sanitizer at the entrance, and I'm giving away hand sanitizers with the company's logo to all my clients. I guess that's the best we can do right now."

"Right…ugh. Anyways Jacob, let's change the subject how was your day?"

"It was good! Thanks! Just sold a house to this couple who moved from Iowa, so I'm just finishing up their paperwork. I can't wait to see you in a few weeks."

"Me too, baby! I have a busy week coming up, but I can call you at night when I'm back in the hotel." I blew him a kiss through the phone, and we hung up.

Tomorrow was my preparation day. I had to get everything together for the Calypso drop, as well as get my work bag together. The first route was to back to LA, and I'd only be spending a night there before jumping on a flight late afternoon. I had just enough time for the drop, and a little bit to spare. Every time I went to LA, I couldn't help but think about him. I mean, it wasn't a constant thought, but I would have a few moments.

Then, it would pass. Besides visiting my dealer, I would stop by and visit Mary and Angela, two sisters I became friends with a while back through a mutual friend. They lived in the hills and the view from their backyard was ridiculous. It was so whimsical, with lights, and beautiful greenery. Not to mention they had a hot tub lined with Himalayan salt. A perfect oasis. They found me fascinating with the *bad girl* life I had. It was fun to hang out with them. They were both really smart women, and both were accountants at a major law firm in Los Angeles.

It was the first day of March. Pre-spring weather. Or should I say, pre- summer? March is one of those months that just drags, and April goes along with it. I started the day with an unexpectedly delicious protein shake, along with an English muffin, smothered with butter and strawberry jam. I had breakfast on my porch in my silk robe and fluffy slippers, and had a few hours to relax before I headed to the airport. I double-checked my stuff, spoke to my Mom on the phone, and got myself ready to go. Just as it was time to head out, Jacob called me. We spoke briefly, but I had to rush. He said he would call me tonight at the hotel. When I arrived at the airport, I did my usual to get to my gate.

When I got there, my co-workers were hanging out, so I said hello to everyone and grabbed a snack in the lounge area. The weather was great today and in LA. Then our captains arrived, so now it was time to board and do our pre-check stuff before we welcomed passengers. About an hour later, we were on the runway ready to take off it wasn't a full flight so that was a good thing. I've been lucky with that lately. The plane gained momentum and off we went. The sky was a bright blue and the clouds were so soft and wispy.

Once we got into proper cruising altitude, it was time to start meal and snack service. Once that was done, I got back into my jumper seat. There was Wi-Fi, so I checked my phone for any new messages, and got caught up on social media for a bit. Before I knew it, we were doing trash collection and last-minute preps for landing. It was about 9 PM in LA when we landed, and I jumped onto the shuttle bus back to my hotel. I was back out on a 5 PM flight tomorrow to San Diego, but I'd be working that flight with Desi, so I was looking forward to it.

I got to my hotel room and decided to call Jacob while I took a shower. He loved when I did stuff like that and, oddly, it made me feel safer. Something about being alone and naked in a hotel shower is not the most comforting thing. I told him I was gonna hang out with Mary and Angela, he told me to have a good time and be safe and to call him when I got back to my hotel. So cute. I looked super LA tonight. The style out here was very different from Miami, but I love to explore fashion! Mary and Angela's place was about forty-five minutes away, but the drive was worth it when I arrived to them both opening the door and handing me a glass of wine, with side hugs from each of them. We headed out to their dreamy backyard and, even though I missed the sunset, their beautiful lighting made up for it. We munched on all sorts of yummy snacks and went through two bottles of wine, just chatting away catching up on each other's lives. It was about four months since I'd seen the girls and, as soon as I filled them in on Jacob, they were extremely happy for me and we drank to that. We decided to get in the hot tub. This wasn't just your ordinary spa tub, did I mention it was lined with Himalayan salt? They added a huge CBD bath bomb and, as we soaked into the bath, I felt my muscles and my mind relaxing. We hung out in there for about an hour and, when I came out, I was feeling so loose and sleepy that the girls offered me their extra guest room. I figured I would spend the night, wake up in the morning go to my hotel, grab Calypso, meet with my dealer, and then head back to the hotel. I texted Jacob goodnight and, within minutes, I was asleep.

I awoke to the smell of coffee. I wasn't a coffee drinker, but the smell was refreshing. Mary was up toasting some bagels, and she had tea ready for me.

"How did you sleep, Vic?" Mary said, handing me a steaming mug of peppermint tea.

"I slept well, Mary! Thank you!" I chirped, before taking a long sip from the mug, "But I should be heading out soon, I have to do a few things before I leave later."

I finished my tea and my bagel called my taxi and gave Mary a hug.

"Tell your sleepy sister bye and I'll see you guys soon again."

As I headed back to the hotel, I texted my dealer to head over to my hotel. Who was I kidding, I didn't feel like leaving again! And who's the boss here anyway? Me! As I was arriving at my hotel, so was Marco. It was always so nice to see him and his kind smile. He came up to my room, I gave him Calypso, and he gave me my profit. We chatted for a few minutes, just shooting the shit until he left. I still had some time before I had to head to the airport where I'd meet Desi before the San Diego flight. Luckily it was a short flight, but it would fly by regardless with Desi's company. I would just be spending the night there, then doing the last leg of my work flight to Atlanta, and back to Miami the same day. I got myself together and ready to go and decided to take a little walk around the outside of the hotel: I still had time to kill. The hotel had a nice little walking path that I'd found one of the many times I'd stayed here on various work trips. I went back to the room, grabbed my stuff, and waited for the shuttle. Once I arrived at the airport, Desi was waiting for me outside.

"Hey, Vic! What are you doing here?" she laughed.

"Let's get this short flight over with so we can have dinner when we get there," I grumbled, feigning frustration.

We got to our gate and boarded the plane. It was just Desi and I servicing this flight since the plane was pretty small. The passengers boarded and we did our usual checklist, made sure everyone was seated and ready to go. Just like that, we were in the air. We had about an hour flight time, so there wasn't any cart service unless there was a request. Desi and I sat in our seats and chatted about what we wanted for dinner in San Diego. I wanted pasta, she wanted burgers. Opposites attract, I guess.

We checked in to our rooms, did a quick change, and headed to the hotel lobby. There was a gorgeous-looking restaurant in the hotel that satisfied both of our cravings. I ordered a coconut mojito and Desi ordered a piña colada. This is what we loved about our job - eating dinner in a completely different state for the night. After dinner, we decided to take a walk. I also stopped by a gift shop and picked out this cool shot glass I knew my Mom would like. I also picked up a San Diego shirt for Jacob, and a key chain for me. I was really into collecting keychains from all my travels. We headed back to the hotel to hang out. Desi was leaving in the morning back to Miami and I had one more flight to Atlanta, but I would be heading home the same day. I was ready to be back home in my cozy bed before tomorrow's hectic schedule. We chilled in my room for a little bit before she left back to her room. I had a really nice bathtub in my room, perfect to take a bubble bath. I rinsed it down, pumped it full of the rosy hotel soap, and filled it up. I soaked down and put on some soft music. Just as I was getting comfortable, my phone began to ring. Mi amor! When I answered, his eyes widened.

"Oh, what is this?" he said, surprised and smirking.

"Well, I had to take the opportunity!" I giggled.

I told Jacob about my day before giving him a little show which he very much enjoyed. What a tease I am. He told me briefly about his day, and we talked about how much we missed each other. It wasn't that I didn't trust our commitment, it was just that I missed him. I missed his physical company, but I knew it wasn't going to last forever. We would be back in each other's arms, and it would feel like we never left. We kissed through the phone and hung up. I soaked a little more before getting out and wrapping myself in the fluffy hotel robe. I turned on the TV but, within minutes, I had fallen asleep. I got up early in the morning to get some breakfast before the flight, headed back to the airport. The flight to Atlanta went smoothly and, after waiting for about two hours in the lounge, it was time to re-board and get home to Miami.

After what felt like an eternity, I was finally pulling up to my house. I was so tired and didn't know what I wanted to do first: shower, eat, or smoke. I decided to eat first - I was starving. I had the next three days off and I was going to enjoy it. It was still a little over two weeks before Jacob was visiting, and I couldn't wait. After my shower, I had a bolt of energy and I was wide awake. I decided to get some chores done around the house and, of course, talk to Jacob. He didn't pick up the first time but then, moments later, he called back. He had a look of concern on his handsome face.

"What's wrong, baby?" I said, heart racing.

"Hey, Vic. I just got some crazy news about that virus, COVID-19."

"Oh gosh, it has a name now?" I exclaimed

"Yes it does and it's getting worse." Jacob's voice was rattled.

"Why are you so worried, Jacob..."

“Well, there’s a lot of talk of things getting shut down, including flights. I mean… everything.”

“No way. They couldn’t do that, could they?”

We both looked at each other in silence.

“Well, um, let’s just try to stay positive and look forward to seeing each other.”

“I miss you so much, amor.”

I hung up with Jacob and melted into my couch. I didn’t dare to look anything up, it would only take me down a nasty rabbit hole. I put on some music, rolled a joint up, and enjoyed it on my porch looking up at the night sky. I was immediately sleepy after that and, by then, it was about 2 AM. I crawled into bed, put on my white noise machine, and snuggled into my jersey knitted sheets.

I woke up at 11 AM to three missed calls from Jacob, four from Desi, and three work emails that said *URGENT.* I shot up in bed and went into panic mode. I rubbed my eyes and called Desi.

“Omg, you’re finally awake.” Desi sighed, out of breath.

“What’s going on, Desi?”

"You haven't read the emails yet?"

"No…why?"

"They're canceling major flights and putting everyone on standby. Everything is shutting down. I can't believe this is happening."

I was speechless and I put her on speaker so I could read the emails.

"So, it says here, we will receive partial payments until further notice and that they anticipate at least four weeks off."

What the hell was going on? Jacob was calling me again, so I said I'd call Desi back and I rang him.

"Hey, babe!" he said, with a sort of urgency I hadn't heard from him before. "Where have you been?"

"I was sleeping and my phone was on silent. Are you okay?"

"Well, not really. My agency is closing for the next few weeks."

I became all fidgety. "I know. I'm off for the next few weeks too. This is crazy, Jacob. I'm scared."

There was a moment of silence

"Hello? You still there?"

"Yeah, baby," Jacob said in a low voice.

My phone started buzzing again, it was my Mom.

"Hey, my mom is calling me. I'll call you back."

I switched over and answered.

"Hey, Mom."

"Mija, are you watching news?" she said, worriedly. When Mom was worried, that's when I knew something was truly up. "Everything is getting shut down. I'm coming over."

I didn't even have a moment to say okay before she hung up. I turned on the TV and I could not believe what I was seeing. A massive worldwide shut down. This was like a nightmare, but everyone was awake, and there was nothing that could wake us up. I realized that Jacob may not be able to come. What was I going to do now? A huge majority of flights were canceled, I had no work for a few weeks. Everything I could possibly imagine was closing, besides essentials. Just then, I heard a knock. It was my Mom, and she had a look of worry on her face. I told her to grab a glass of wine and sit. Pandemonium was setting in. Being in limbo was an awful feeling.

CHAPTER SIX

Lifeless

It had been one week since the news and the word around town was a total lockdown. Clubs and lounges had closed, all restaurants and fast food closed for indoor dining, and some weren't even open at all. Nail salons and the gyms were closed and, well, the only thing open was the grocery store, and the store down the street had limited hours. Today, I had no choice but to go grocery shopping. I was down to one egg and half of a bottle of water and some random expired things in my pantry. I heard that the grocery store was letting people in with certain limitations and there was a sign that said only two people were allowed in. Not to mention we had to wear a mask covering our noses and mouths and stay six feet apart. Desi wanted to go with me, she needed a few things too, so Josh drove us and waited in the car. We arrived in the parking lot, there were about twenty people in line. We each grabbed a cart, put on our masks, and got in line. A few minutes later they let about ten people in and, before long, it was our turn. As we entered the grocery store, a wave of sadness came over me. I stood, frozen, looking at everyone with masks covering their faces. I began to tear up. This felt so weird. A few weeks ago, everyone was casually grocery shopping. Now we are all masked up and following the directions inside the store: no one could go up an aisle that was pointing downward and vice versa. I lost my train of thought, but I knew I had to get it together - I didn't want to be in here long. Desi and I split up. I got down to business and grabbed what I needed. There was a limit on paper towels and toilet paper, but it didn't matter - there was none on the shelf. I'm not sure what people thought hogging the toilet paper and paper towels would do in this situation. I made it to the check-out, and Desi was right behind me. I packed my stuff and waited for her. We walked out together, and I ripped the mask off my face. We both doused our hands down with sanitizer which stung my skin. I would definitely try to make this food last - I wasn't looking for another trip any time soon.

I had just finished putting away the last bit of my groceries when Jacob called me. He was supposed to come out in about a week, but there was a halt to that. There were no flights. Everything was extremely limited. I thought that meant that we were about to be separated for who knows how long; but he suggested he would just drive out here. It was the safest option but, I mean, the drive was no picnic. But we missed each other.

Not only that, but he was also going to stay for two whole weeks, which would be interesting considering there wasn't much we could actually do. We would be spending some *real* quality time together and I really could use his company right now. Everything that was going on was changing daily. Everyone was just in a state of limbo. I tried to avoid the news. I knew it would only make me panic more. My main goal was to stay safe and healthy. Everyone was so scared to be close to one another. My mom was changing her clothes at the door and Desi was traveling with a thermometer and sanitizer. There was talk that even cats could get it as there was a confirmed case in a zoo on one of their tigers. It was times like this I missed Lucy. She went to kitty heaven a few months ago, it was still too painful to talk about. Her ashes were on a single nightstand, with a few pictures, and her paw print. I still wasn't ready for a fur baby yet. I felt guilty even thinking about it. When the majority of the city gets shut down and you currently aren't working, you have a lot of time to sit and think. I was so eager for Jacob to come.

As the days passed, my nails needed care. Since the nail salons were closed, I went to the neighborhood store and did what most girls were doing right now, I purchased a gel nail kit. This should be interesting. Every woman in the area must have had the same idea because I was lucky to get a kit at all. It was the last one. The shelves were empty. I mean, everything that had to do with nails was empty, not to mention the false eyelashes completely gone. I was lucky I had a few sets at home. I decided to pamper myself – wine and nails. Jacob called me as he was driving.

“Hey, amor! How are you?” he said with a grin.

“I’m good, baby! Just going to attempt to do my nails and have a glass of wine.”

“Good luck!” he giggled.

“So, where you driving to?” I asked.

He gave me a look and a smirk before saying, “On my way to you.”

“Excuse me?” I blurted out, “Baby! You weren’t supposed to leave for another three days!”

“Well, I had the opportunity, so I’m coming! I’m still really far, I’ve only been driving for an hour. I should be there tomorrow early noon, I don’t plan on stopping.”

“Oh my gosh, are you sure Jacob? You can’t drive straight through! You should stop at a rest area and take a nap.”

“Okay, if I get tired babe, I’ll stop and take a nap. I promise. I can’t wait to see you.”

We hung up so he could listen to music and concentrate on driving. Oh my God. He was driving all that way, through the night, in the middle of a pandemic, for me. Well, it was time to get polished up! A full body scrub, paint my toes, and hope that my fingernails would come out nicely. After I finished doing my self-care, I decided to clean up the house a little. I decided to call Desi and my Mom to give them a heads up and soon it was getting late. I called Jacob to check on him and told him to call me any time if he needed anything, and that I couldn't wait to see him. Off to bed, I went. It was raining a little and the noise put me right to sleep. I woke up around 10 AM to Jacob calling me. He said he would be at my house before 12 PM. Poor thing, he sounded exhausted. But, I had a few things to cheer him up as soon as he arrived, and one of those things was me.

I got up and got myself together. I lit some candles to make the house smell delicious and ordered tacos for his arrival. Before I knew it, he was pulling up into my driveway. He got out a did a big stretch and I ran to him. He swept me up off the ground and kissed me. I already felt so much safer in his company. Everything felt less scary in his arms. Jacob walked into the house and kicked off his shoes.

“I really gotta shower and get into some fresh clothes, mi amor”

I gave him a fresh towel and let him do his thing. When he got out of the shower, the food had arrived and there was a delicious spread of food on the table waiting for him. We were in taco heaven and we indulged in everything. By the end, we were stuffed like cheese ravioli.

“That was perfect babe, thank you”

We went to the living room to relax and chat about everything. Jacob was still kind of working, remotely. Mostly on houses that he was closing right before things shut down. As for me, I told him I was on reserve and would be getting only part of my paycheck until further notice. We brainstormed some outdoor things we could do that would be safe and I mentioned going on a boat ride up and down the canal. I decided I’d call tomorrow for pricing and to schedule a ride. It would be so nice to be out on the water, enjoying the beautiful view and sun.

I woke up to Jacob softly rubbing my back. I could only assume what that meant! I excused myself to the bathroom, brushed my teeth, washed my face, and rubbed some almond oil on my skin. The smell was so sensual and relaxing. I returned to the bed and slipped off my nightgown. I loved my naked skin against his, and I loved his smell. I ran my hand through his thick, black hair, and gazed into his big, beautiful eyes. We kissed as he massaged my hips and lower back. Soon enough, the covers were on the floor, and we were in pleasurable bliss for twenty perfect minutes. I rolled over to drink some water and stretch, and Jacob got up to make us some grilled cheese sandwiches. After breakfast, we jumped in the shower together where I couldn't help but tease him a little.

"Careful, amor, I'm not on birth control."

He gripped me up tighter and whispered back, "That makes it harder to stay away from you."

Afterward, I sat on my bed, with my comfy robe, and my hair in a towel. The weather looked beautiful today, so I called the boat company. They had an amazing price - go figure! With the shutdown, I'm sure they needed business. They had an opening for 2 PM for ninety minutes. I hung up and we began to get ready.

We arrived at the dock where the boat was waiting for us. It was all black, and really stood out among the other ones. Our captain greeted with a kind smile underneath his mask and informed us that everything had been wiped down and sanitized and that there was a cooler of refreshments, including Champagne, and a delicious tray of assorted veggies and cheeses. It was perfect. We started our journey up the canal. I felt so safe out here. So much ocean. Not to mention the beautiful houses we floated by. I decided to mess around and randomly wave to people. Jacob and I laughed, kissed, and talked about life as we passed house after house. I saw two little boys, playing together in what looked like an empty, mosaic marble swimming pool. How peaceful they both seemed, and, at the same time, I wondered *sheesh! What did their parents do for a living?* I popped the Champagne, and Jacob I did a toast. Then, the captain turned on some music for us, and Jacob pulled me up to dance with him in the breeze. With the wind through my hair, and the sun shining on my skin, my thoughts were so clear. Sadly, the world was in shambles, but it felt good to just forget about the uncertainty for a little.

There were other boats out here doing the same, and we waved to them in solidarity. It was nice to see that other people were trying to live their lives in this abnormal reality too. The ninety minutes passed so quickly and, before I knew it, we were docking up. We thanked the captain and left him a nice tip. I felt so relaxed, and I was ready to go home with Jacob and make some dinner. I was in the mood to make lasagna - one of my specialties - with some homemade garlic bread.

When we got home, I slipped into a little more something comfortable and popped open a bottle of wine for my love and me. I started on the lasagna while Jacob handled some business for his job on his laptop. The house smelled divine, and soon dinner was ready, so I put on some music and set the table. Just then, the doorbell rang. I looked at Jacob, confused. I walked to the door only to see my Mom, and I became a little nervous.

"Mom! Hi! Are you okay?"

"Mija, hi! I called you three times and you didn't pick up," she said, relieved as though I was a missing person. "I was worried, so came over."

I had forgotten my phone was still in my purse, which was on my bed. Obviously, Mom would be eating dinner with us now, which was perfectly fine. Mom didn't have an issue with Jacob. I set another place at the table, we said grace, and I began to serve everyone. Mom and Jacob were chatting like they'd known each other forever, and I couldn't stop grinning. Two of my favorite people truly hitting it off!

"Victoria, this is really good!" my Mom said.

"Thanks, Mom! I learn from the best!"

After dinner, Mom made some coffee and we all hung out in the living room. We told her about our boat ride and how peaceful it was. She stayed for another hour and then left to go home. Jacob, like the true gentleman he is, walked her to her car and gave her a hug. So cute. It was really nice having him. Although the world was chaotic, my heart was content. I felt safe. We crawled into bed, and I laid my head on his chest and listened to his heart beating, while he stroked my hair so tenderly.

Jacob drifted off to sleep within minutes. It amazed me how fast he could fall asleep. I stayed up for about another hour watching TV on my laptop and waiting for my melatonin to kick in.

Jacob was already awake when I woke up and was on the porch, having some coffee. He was on the phone, and I didn't want to be nosey, so I waited for him to finish before heading out there to join him. He looked stern and serious and took a deep breath.

"Well, my love," he said, taking both my hands in his. "I have to cut my trip short and leave after the weekend."

My jaw dropped, "No! Why?"

"Even though everything is virtual right now, they need me back in Virginia because I had two houses pending and, well, now they're both closing one day apart. I need to be there in person to finish up a few things. Both commissions are really important."

Damn. What could I possibly say at this point? I was sad, but he had business to handle. I never wanted to be in the way of his accomplishments. I was just glad we had the next three days together.

I just didn't want to be stuck in the house, so we went to the park and had a picnic. I had put together a delicious spread of cheese and cold cuts, some wine, and crackers. We laid out a blanket and put our bare feet down on the grass to ground ourselves - I heard it's relaxing and good for the soul. The park was pretty big, and we could see a few other couples had the same idea. Well, the sun was out, and it was the perfect picnic day. We hung out there for hours, just talking. I could never get tired of his company. We bounced off one another like no one I'd ever met, except maybe Desi; but Jacob had things that Desi definitely couldn't offer me.

We decided to head back to my place. The moment we stepped inside, I slipped off my dress and passionately kissed him. He picked me up and carried me to the bedroom, where he laid me on the bed. I couldn't get enough of him. Afterward, I rolled a joint and went to the living room to smoke. Jacob ordered us a dinner of steak and shrimp, with mashed potatoes, and salad - what a perfect Friday night. After dinner, we put on a movie, and I threw some chocolate chip cookies in the oven. I didn't want the night to end, and neither did he. After the movie, we decided to sit on the porch and look at the stars. We sat there, enjoying each other's company until three in the morning. Suddenly, out of the blackness, I saw a shooting star. I closed my eyes, tight, and made a wish. I hoped, more than anything, it would come true. We slunk into bed and cuddled up together. This time, I was the first one asleep. The rest of the weekend was spent playing cards, drinking wine, and enjoying each other's bodies and company; but, before we knew it, Monday had come. Jacob was packed and ready to go. On his last morning, we cooked brunch together, and enjoyed our final moments, at last for now. I walked him to his car, holding back tears. He wrapped me up in a hug and kissed me goodbye, and off he went. *What was I going to do with myself now?* I wondered.

What were other people doing to stay sane? I sat on the couch and cried until I was all cried out, and then called Desi to ask if she wanted to come over. I didn't want to be alone. Who really wanted to be alone during this chaotic time?

CHAPTER SEVEN

País de los sueños

It's been six months since the pandemic started. I spent about seven weeks at home before things started to slightly open up in the city, and I took two weeks off to go to Virginia to visit Jacob. We were still going strong, and we really helped each other the last few months. Because of that, we became closer. I had the opportunity to return to work but honestly, I'm not sure if I'm ready. There were mixed feelings because of the mixed reviews I'd heard about the working conditions from other flight attendants. As for Calypso, I was only seeing my local dealer, but the revenue was still decent. I picked up new hobbies like baking and coloring books for adults. As much as I wanted to feel normal, I felt like I was in a dreamland. This was our new normal. Rules and regulations on everything were always changing. Sadly, Desi and her boyfriend decided to take some type apart, so she was spending a lot of time at my house. We had our nightly routine that usually consisted of two bottles of wine and a quick game of rock papers scissors to see who was cooking or paying for takeout, followed by facials. Jacob would usually call me around the same time every night so we would chat for a little. I always looked forward to seeing his face and hearing his voice, even though the distance hurt. Then, I would have my nightly joint and, sometimes, even Desi would even take a hit. This pandemic had people doing things that they would probably never do, and it definitely brought your loved ones closer. I felt better when Desi would sleep over I wasn't alone, and it was even better when Mom would join in – she'd always insist on cooking for us, playing cards and board games, and taking care of us both.

I decided that I was going to take some more time off work. Financially, I could still afford it. Today, I decided to go into my back yard and do some grounding. I think a lot of people were trying new things out, and I'd read about grounding before, so I went to the yard, found a nice spot in the sun, and removed my socks. I just stood there connecting with Mother Earth. The sun beamed on me with pleasurable warmth on my skin. After I did that for about fifteen minutes, I laid down my yoga mat and did some stretching. I had a lemon tree in my backyard I just loved looking at, not to mention the beautiful lemons it grew for me. Maybe that would be my next little hobby - plant some more citrus fruit. Sometimes I missed being able to go to a lounge and have a drink but, honestly, things were so sketchy right now. Not to mention crime had gone up. On my social media, some of my coworkers and friends had no issue stepping back out into the night life; but, for me, it was way too risky. It was best to stay home and avoid that type of activity for now. Besides, it didn't feel the same anymore. I wasn't sure if it would ever feel or be the same. No one wanted to get this virus, and with the diverse opinions of the media, it was a terrifying world to be in. Although, you would hear of some people bouncing back quickly, there were the ones that fought a good fight but went home to heaven. This virus was an uncomfortable conversation that no one wanted to have. Everyone had their opinions and theories on everything that was going on which was causing tensions between friends and family and lots of protest all over the world. Thankfully, I had my small group of people who I loved and cared about, and we were all on the same page. Everyone seemed to have become health gurus, too. I mean, everywhere I scrolled, people were posting teas, and herbs, and vitamins to take to build your immune system. I liked to imagine my immune system to be this tough little fighter who was ready for war, ready to defend my body.

Now that I knew I was going to take at least six more weeks off work, I wanted to build some type of schedule for myself, just to keep some sanity in my life. I sat on my bed with a whiteboard and a big marker, planning my days in bright colored pen, when I heard my phone ring. It was Jacob calling me!

"Hey babe!" I could hear his excitement through the phone already. "How are you today?"

"Hi baby! I'm good, just sitting on my bed trying to build some kind of schedule."

He giggled, "How about you open the door? I think there's something outside for you."

My heart jumped as I leaped up to get to the door. I imagined dinner, or some flowers, but could not have been happier with what was waiting for me. Standing on my doorstep wan my Jacob.

"Mi amor!" I screeched as I dove into his embrace, "What are you doing here?"

"Well, I have a few days off and I was missing you, so I decided to…fly in."

My jaw dropped. We had made the decision to stick to only driving to see each other to avoid getting sick or any hassles as there was plenty of tension in the sky. Every day it seemed like I was watching videos or hearing stories of crazy incidents happening on flights. That was another reason why I decided not to return to work. I was upset.

"Babe, don't be mad. I wore a mask, and I was the only one in my row. It was an easy ride, I couldn't stand to do all that driving, and I really really missed you."

He knew that would get me. With that smile, and his arms around me after weeks of separation, how could I stay mad?

"Come in and go change your clothes, silly."

After we made up for lost time in the bedroom, we both slipped into a cozy slumber. I awoke feeling so content and peaceful, still wrapped up in Jacobs arms. I think the key to keeping the chaos out is to build serenity all around you. I had to tell Desi our sleep overs were canceled for a few days, but she understood and said I owed her tacos. Fair deal considering how much we both loved tacos! Jacob was coming out of the bathroom as I slipped my clothes back on.

"How would you feel about trying to go out tonight and eat out at a restaurant? Outside, of course."

I was hesitant. I really wasn't sure how I felt about it. I didn't really have an interest in going out anymore, and I had this looming anxiety about being out of my comfort space. There must be a name for what I was feeling, there's no way I could be the only one.

"Please, honey?" Jacob said, "Let's just find something low key! And if you don't like it, we can leave. I just miss reality, you know?"

Reluctantly, I said yes and started to get ready. This should be interesting.

We found ourselves walking to the strip to see if we could find a place I was comfortable to eat in. It was still kind of early, so I figured we could miss the chaotic dinner rush. Luckily, we found this adorable Cuban restaurant with comfy outside dining.

"How do you feel, mi amor? Is this good?"

I smiled and nodded again. Something that was so normal was now so awkward. I whipped out my hand sanitizer and put it on the table – I wasn't taking any chances. Our waiter approached us wearing a bright green mask. The only way I could tell he was smiling was because his eyes got squinty as he introduced himself. We ordered some cocktails and appetizers to start off which we nibbled for the next forty-five minutes. When Jacob and I talked, the world disappeared around us and, before we knew it, it was time to order. As the world around us came back into focus, I realized the restaurant was suddenly packed. Jacob could see the tension in my eyes, and we ordered our food to go.

Leaving the restaurant, I felt relieved, but ridiculously annoyed that I even felt this way. Though, I was grateful that Jacob was keeping an eye on me, and that my wellbeing was at the front of his mind. On our walk home, there was a light warm breeze that felt like butterflies against my skin. We held hands and just chatted.

"Babe, things will get better." Jacob said, as though he could predict the future.

I shrugged my shoulders and said, "Will it?"

As I opened the door to my house, relief rushed over me. I changed into comfy clothes and lit some candles. The food was yummier without the stressful environment, I was happy we were at home eating. After dinner, we had some coffee which, for some reason, always makes me sleepy, which left Jacob alone for the night. Or so I thought.

I awoke at 2 AM to find him still awake on his laptop, working in the living room.

"Hey you!" He whispered, turning down the brightness on his screen to save my sleepy eyes, "You passed out after the coffee."

“I know, ugh, sorry!” I said, sleepily, “What are you still doing awake?”

“I’m just doing some stuff for work. Couldn’t really sleep, my whole schedule is off.”

I cuddled in next to him and scrolled on my phone while he typed away. Before I knew it, it was 3:30 AM.

“Baby, we should get some sleep.” I whispered.

He turned off his laptop and rubbed his eyes, “Babe I want to talk to you about something tomorrow and, before you jump to anything, its nothing bad at all, okay?”

He kissed me on my forehead and called me his muñeca. As I tried to drift off to sleep, I couldn’t help but run through every possible version of what he might want to say to me.

I woke up first in the morning to freshen myself and start some coffee. I guess Jacob could smell the coffee because moments later he was shirtless in his boxers in the kitchen, rubbing sleep from his eyes.

“Well, hello there, Mister!” I said with a grin, “I’m surprised you aren’t sleeping in considering how late you stayed up last night.”

We both sat on the patio enjoying our coffee, and I was just waiting for him to start talking. My mind was whirring. After a few moments of silence, he cleared his throat.

"So, Victoria, I've been thinking about something and I'm just going to come out and say it."

Oh God, what is it? A breakup? A proposal?

"I love you and I think we should move in together."

Oh. My. God!

"I'm moving back to Miami if that means being with you."

I was totally stunned, and my stomach was doing flips. I sure wish now he had waited until I had more than coffee in me.

"Are you serious, baby?" I said as I jumped up and hugged him. "So I'm assuming that's a yes?" he giggled.

"So, what do you have in mind?" I asked.

"Well babe, I'm thinking we can make this happen in about a month. I've been looking at places."

He pulled out his laptop and revealed a gorgeously organized spreadsheet, filled with plenty of options that weren't too far from where I lived already. I could only wonder how long he'd been thinking about this and whether he was scared to ask. We spent the next hour talking about the plans. This was going to be a big transition, but I was ready and excited.

Jacob was leaving tomorrow to start packing his things and to put his place on the market. He said he would narrow down some places we could pick from, and I trusted we were in good hands. I was so excited to tell my Mom and Desi. I know this was a big change, but I felt really happy considering how unsettled the last few months have been. In a world that had become so divided, I wanted to work on my bubble of happiness and keep all that tyranny out. Now my bubble had expanded, and I couldn't be happier. I emailed my landlord and gave him a formal update and time frame I would be moving out. He was happy for me but sad that I was leaving because I had been such a good tenant over the last five years. I wanted a pool, that would be such a nice change. Or a hot tub. Or maybe even both! I had lots to do in preparation for the move, like donating some of my furniture and keeping a good number of things. Jacob said he would bring some things from his place and whatever else we needed we would choose together. Jacob was happy he was moving back to Miami. Now he'd get to be close to his family, and they were excited about the news. Also, there would be more room for me to grow Calypso! I wasn't too sure about how dedicated I was now to staying a flight attendant, considering how well my product was selling, but I had some time to think about it. Jacob had a flight leaving in the early afternoon, so we spent the day dreaming about what type of house we wanted, the area we wanted to be in, how we wanted to decorate the place, and so much more. I was on this gigantic cloud with him, and nothing could take us down.

Five weeks later, following plenty of house tours, we pulled it off. We moved into our new home, and it was absolutely dreamy. I wasn't too far from my Mom or Desi, and Jacob was near his family. The house had been remodeled and had all new appliances. It was a three-bedroom, so we had plenty of space, and it was all beautifully tiled which is my favorite style, mostly because it was easier to keep clean. And how can I forget the best part…we had a pool *and* a small hot tub! I was so excited to decorate everything. We had a beautiful palm tree in the front of the house which swayed delicately in the Miami breeze. It was just so perfect, I had to pinch myself. There was no need to throw a housewarming party; besides, the two most important people, Mom and Desi, came over for our first Sunday dinner. Mom blessed the kitchen as she always does and prepared a delicious meal. The kitchen had a big, marble island in the middle that was so big I could dance on it if I wanted to. The world may be falling apart, but my world was strong and resilient. Everyone I loved was right here with me. I had a hard choice to make, and the time had come. I had about a week before I was due to return to work and, well, it was either go back or resign. I sat with my thoughts as I soaked in a hot, lavender bubble bath. Desi decided she would be returning, but you had to wear a mask and there was talk of a vaccine that you had to eventually get to stay safe and keep working. It didn't feel right that the years of my life I dedicated to being a flight attendant was over, but maybe it was time for me to move on. I had my business with Calypso, but a lot would change on how I would get my products to my dealers. I had options which was good no matter what. I guess there are always options in life; you may not like them, but at least they're there.

Regardless, I know I had support with whatever decision I made, and that made me feel good. So, the next few days I was going to take the time to reflect before sending out that life-changing email.

It was a peaceful day in my house and, little by little, things were coming together, and it was beginning to feel like home. I decided to sit by the pool and write out my thoughts. The sun was beautiful, and I was enjoying a wine spritzer while I tanned. The sky was blue, not a cloud in the sky. Jacob was out setting up his new office space. I had Calypso all set up in the spare room which we would use as a guest room, or for the nights I wanted to sleep alone - especially on my PMS days. Jacob and I talked about how important it was to give each other personal space when needed, and I really appreciated his understanding of my independent spirit. As the day went on, my decision was becoming clearer. It was time to move on. I would always cherish everything about my flight attendant career, but I could feel that it was time to build my Calypso empire into something bigger because it had potential and was already proving it.

Jacob jokingly said the other night that, if I wanted to get into real estate, he could enroll me in courses that would be an interesting career change. But, for now, it was time to tell everyone my decision. First up was Desi, and I was nervous. It would break my heart if she was sad, but she was excited for me, despite losing her flying buddy. Mom was stopping over later so I would tell her then and, as for Jacob, well I had a little something special planned later in the night. I composed the email but decided to hold off on clicking send until I'd heard everyone's opinion. Mom eventually arrived bearing chicken salads for us to enjoy. I didn't want to waste time so, as soon as she sat down, I told her. She was actually happy I was leaving! She said there were too many incidents happening on flights nowadays and she would be worried. She gave me a hug and kiss and congratulated me on my decision. Jacob arrived home as Mom was leaving. Jacob's uncle, Ricardo, was taking her out for dinner! It was crazy how they were still talking to each other since they meet on New Year's Eve, and I was so happy for her. I told Jacob dinner was going to be something light because of the late-night activity I had planned for us. If he ate too much, he would fall asleep early – I guess I know him pretty well! I made us quesadillas with the works and opened a bottle of wine. After dinner, I told Jacob to get into his swimming trunks and meet me by the hot tub. I changed the outdoor lights to an ocean blue, and I waited for him in my bikini with a platter of strawberries.

As we soaked our bodies in the warm water, the blue glow of the lights illuminated our faces.

"This is the life!" Jacob said, splashing me playfully with the water, "So, babe what's up?"

"Ok…well…I've made up my mind," his eyes grew more concerned, "I'm resigning from the airline and focusing on Calypso and, well, I want to get into the real estate business if you'd be my teacher?"

He came close to me and kissed me. "I'm happy for you, babe. It's going to be good for you! And I need my lady on the ground not in the skies."

We chatted about my future, and our future together, and Jacob offered to massage my feet. I lifted my feet out of the water, and he tenderly worked his fingers into my skin. Before long, the massage started going up my legs, and I then wrapped both of my legs around his waist. The jets of the hot tub massaged my back, as I slipped off my bikini. There was undeniable passion between us was out of this world. We got out, showered, changed, and got into bed. I had my email ready to be sent in the morning and felt so content about everything. I kept my mind off the chaos the world was enduring and was focused on this new chapter in my life.

I woke up feeling the most refreshed I'd felt in forever. Jacob started to squirm around and stretch, before grabbing my waist and whispering *good morning*. We got out of bed and got ourselves ready. Thank God there were two bathrooms, I'm sure women out there know what I mean. I still wanted to keep some things to myself, and not reveal my good, bad, and ugly all at once. I sat at the table with my coffee and laptop and prepared the email. 1...2. 3…sent! My eyes welled up, and Jacob came over and hugged me.

"I just can't believe that part of my life is actually over!"

I took a deep breath in and decided to go tend to my plants. About an hour later I received an email back. It was formal, but they mentioned they were sad to see me go and wished me well. This flight attendant was checking out, sayonara!

As I reflect on these last few months, I'm painfully aware that it wasn't just me that was thrown into change - it was the whole world. Nothing was the same. Anyone you spoke to could tell you the mental and physical changes the pandemic had caused in their lives. Thankfully for me, it played out softly and I was grateful. I understand that I will have my bad days, maybe weeks, maybe years, just like anyone else; but I learned to be much more grateful for everything I had and the people in my life. All of us would be a part of history, and sixty years from now when many of us aren't around anymore, our stories will have been told. And people who remember and knew those who lived through this will be able to pass those stories on. But, for now, this was my new reality. I had to stay strong because this was far from being over but, despite it all, I had faith and optimism. Not everything was filled with negativity and bad, there was greener grass on the other side. My glass was full, and, for that, this pandemonium was somehow bitterly sweet.

Read the previous two books
in the *Victoria's Highway* series now, or listen to the
audiobook versions on Audible, narrated by Deana Taheri.